This Book Belongs To

_____

® Landoll, Inc.
© 1996 Landoll, Inc.
Ashland, Ohio 44805

Santa's Favorite Storybook

TABLE OF CONTENTS

The Twelve Days of Christmas

Classic Holiday Collection

written by Dandi
illustrated by Tammie Speer-Lyon

On the first day of Christmas,
My true love gave to me, a partridge in a pear tree.

On the second day of Christmas,
My true love gave to me,
Two turtle doves,
And a partridge in a pear tree.

On the third day of Christmas, my true love gave to me,
Three French hens, two turtle doves,
And a partridge in a pear tree.

On the fourth day of Christmas,
My true love gave to me,
Four coly birds,
Three French hens,
Two turtle doves,
And a partridge in a pear tree.

On the fifth day of Christmas, my true love gave to me,
Five gold rings!
Four coly birds, three French hens, two turtle doves,
And a partridge in a pear tree.

On the sixth day of Christmas, my true love gave to me,
Six geese a'laying, five gold rings!
Four coly birds, three French hens, two turtle doves,
And a partridge in a pear tree.

On the seventh day of Christmas, my true love gave to me,
Seven swans a'swimming, six geese a'laying, five gold rings!
Four coly birds, three French hens, two turtle doves,
And a partridge in a pear tree.

On the eighth day of Christmas, my true love gave to me,
Eight maids a'milking, seven swans a'swimming,
Six geese a'laying, five gold rings!
Four coly birds, three French hens, two turtle doves,
And a partridge in a pear tree.

On the ninth day of Christmas, my true love gave to me,
Nine ladies dancing, eight maids a'milking,
Seven swans a'swimming, six geese a'laying,
Five gold rings!

Four coly birds,
Three French hens,
Two turtle doves,
And a partridge in
a pear tree.

On the tenth day of Christmas, my true love gave to me,
Ten lords a'leaping, nine ladies dancing,
Eight maids a'milking, seven swans a'swimming,
Six geese a'laying, five gold rings!
Four coly birds, three French hens, two turtle doves,
And a partridge in a pear tree.

On the eleventh day of Christmas, my true love gave to me,
Eleven pipers piping, ten lords a'leeping, nine ladies dancing,
Eight maids a'milking, seven swans a'swimming,
Six geese a'laying, five gold rings!
Four coly birds, three French hens, two turtle doves,
And a partridge in a pear tree.

On the twelfth day of Christmas, my true love gave to me,
Twelve drummers drumming, eleven pipers piping,
Ten lords a'leaping, nine ladies dancing,
Eight maids a'milking, seven swans a'swimming,
Six geese a'laying, five gold rings!

Four coly birds, three French hens, two turtle doves,

And a partridge in a pear tree.

THE STORY OF
SMALL PINE

by Diane Stortz
Illustrated by Mary Lou Faltico

All young pine trees long to grow up straight and tall so they can be Christmas trees when they are older.

Small Pine was more than a little crooked and not tall at all. But even when he was sold for half price at an after-Christmas sale, Small Pine never stopped hoping. "Someday I will be Christmas tree," he said "I know I will."

Small Pine was planted in a corner of the backyard. He learned to be happy there, mostly because of a little boy named John Michael.

On spring days, John Michael sat quietly
and watched a pair of robins make a nest
in Small Pine's branches.

On hot summer days, he lay in
Small Pine's shade to keep cool.

On fall days, he and his puppy Nappy
played ball together in Small Pine's
corner of the backyard.

And on winter days, when soft snow
covered the ground, John Michael
made perfect snow angels all around
Small Pine.

With winter and the first snow, Small Pine knew Christmas would be coming soon. He stood as straight and tall as he possibly could, still hoping that somehow he would be a Christmas tree.

But another taller, straighter tree
stood in John Michael's house, decorated
with lights and ornaments.

On Christmas morning, John Michael tiptoed downstairs. Under the tree were so many presents! But through the window, as the sun was coming up, John Michael saw something even more wonderful.

It was Small Pine, covered with new snow, glistening like a hundred lights. A family of redbirds rested on his branches, and the sun shone like a starburst at the top of the little tree.

"Small Pine, you're a Christmas tree!" said John Michael. Small Pine proudly stood as straight and tall as he possibly could. He was very, very happy!

The Night Before Christmas

by Clement C. Moore

Twas the night before Christmas,
And all through the house
Not a creature was stirring,
Not even a mouse.

The stockings were hung by
The chimney with care,
In hopes that St. Nicholas
Soon would be there.

The children were nestled all snug in their beds,
While visions of sugarplums danced in their heads.

And Ma in her kerchief, and I in my cap,

Had just settled down for a long winter's nap.

When out on the lawn there arose such a clatter,

I sprang from my bed to see what was the matter.

Away to the window I flew like a flash,

Tore open the shutters and threw up the sash.

The moon on the breast of the new-fallen snow,

Gave a luster of midday to objects below.

When, what to my wondering eyes should appear,

But a miniature sleigh, and eight tiny reindeer,

With a little old driver, so lively and quick,

I knew in a moment it must be St. Nick.

59

ore rapid than eagles his coursers they came,
And he whistled, and shouted, and called them by name:

"Now, Dasher! Now, Dancer! Now Prancer and Vixen!
On, Comet! On, Cupid! On, Donner and Blitzen!
To the top of the porch! To the top of the wall!
Now, dash away! Dash away! Dash away all!"

As dry leaves that before the wild hurricane fly,
When they meet with an obstacle, mount to the sky,
So up to the housetop the coursers they flew,
With the sleigh full of toys, and St. Nicholas, too.

And then in a twinkling, I heard on the roof
The prancing and pawing of each little hoof.

63

As I drew in my head, and was turning around,
Down the chimney St. Nicholas came with a bound.

He was dressed all in fur, from his head to his foot,
And his clothes were all tarnished with ashes and soot.
A bundle of toys he had flung on his back,
And he looked like a peddler just opening his pack.

His eyes how they twinkled!
His dimples how merry!
His cheeks were like roses,
His nose like a cherry.
His droll little mouth,
Was drawn up like a bow,
And the beard on his chin,
Was as white as the snow.

The stump of a pipe he held tight in his teeth,
And the smoke, it encircled his head like a wreath.
He had a broad face and a little round belly,
That shook, when he laughed, like a bowl full of jelly.

He was chubby and plump, a right jolly old elf,
And I laughed when I saw him, in spite of myself.
A wink of his eye and a twist of his head,
Soon gave me to know I had nothing to dread.

He spoke not a word, but went straight to his work,
And filled all the stockings, then turned with a jerk,
And laying his finger aside of his nose,
And giving a nod, up the chimney he rose.

He sprang to his sleigh,
To his team gave a whistle,
And away they all flew,
Like the down of a thistle,
And I heard him exclaim,
As he drove out of sight . . .

"Merry Christmas to all, and to all a good night!"

The SNOWMAN POSTMAN

by Andy Rector

Illustrated by Donna Lee

Olund Owl, Cassie Cat, and Rob Rabbit love Christmas. "It's Christmas time," said Olund Owl. "Let's put up a wreath."

"Hurry, hurry," said Cassie Cat. "It's cold outside."

"Let's make pudding," said
Rob Rabbit. "Chocolate pudding!"

"Let's eat the pudding in front
of a fire," said Cassie Cat. "A fire in the
fireplace will keep us nice and warm."

"Let's decorate the tree in my front yard," said Olund Owl. "I have lots of ornaments and a big yellow star."

"I have an idea," said Cassie Cat
"Let's build a snowman. We can make
him a happy snowman."

"I will dress our snowman in my grandpa's old postman uniform," said Rob Rabbit. "We can call him our 'snowman postman'!"

79

"Well, it's been a fun day," said Olund Owl. "But I'm tired. Let's play together tomorrow. Good night."

81

The next day Cassie Cat ran to meet Olund Owl and Rob Rabbit. "Look what I found in my mailbox," said Cassie Cat. "A Christmas card."

83

"My card is from 'The Snowman Postman'." said Cassie Cat.

"Mine, too," said Olund Owl.

"Mine, too," said Rob Rabbit.

"The snowman came to life!"
said Cassie Cat.

"Let's ask our new neighbor if he got
a card, too," said Rob Rabbit.

87

"Surprise!" said Farley Fox. "The cards are really from me. I want to be your friend. Won't you come in for a Christmas treat?"

89

"Merry Christmas, Farley Fox!" said Olund Owl.

And they all ate his wonderful chocolate pudding with snowman cookies.

The NUTCRACKER

Christmas was soon approaching! Clara and her little brother, Fritz, eagerly awaited the presents they hoped to find under the Christmas tree. Clara dreamed of beautiful dolls and Fritz imagined rows and rows of shiny, tin soldiers.

On Christmas Eve, Clara's parents gave a wonderful party. The Christmas tree sparkled and many presents lay beneath it.

The last guest to arrive was Herr Dross-elmeyer, Clara's godfather. Everyone loved him. He was a wonderful toymaker and he told marvelous stories. His toys were so life-like, the children wondered if they were actually real!

As soon as Christmas dinner was finished, the children eagerly unwrapped their gifts.

This Christmas, Herr Drosselmeyer brought Clara a very special present . . . a Nutcracker dressed like a soldier.

"This is my favorite Christmas present!" Clara said with delight.

Fritz glared at the Nutcracker and said, "He's ugly!" He grabbed the Nutcracker from Clara, pushed a nut into his mouth, and slammed it shut. Crack! The Nutcracker's jaw was broken!

Almost in tears, Clara picked up the Nutcracker. "He'll be handsome again in the morning," whispered Herr Drosselmeyer as he tied a handkerchief around the Nutcracker's broken jaw.

Late that night, as the clock struck midnight, Clara tiptoed to the toy room to check on her broken Nutcracker. She was startled . . . Herr Drosselmeyer was sitting on top of the clock while mice scampered across the floor!

The mice seemed larger than life to Clara, as did Fritz's toy soldiers. Soon the toy soldiers and the mice were engaged in battle . . . bugles were blowing and drums were beating!

To Clara's amazement, the Nutcracker came to life, grabbed a sword, and joined the battle. Suddenly, an evil Mouse King wearing a golden crown and carrying a sword, appeared out of the ranks of mice.

As the Mouse King advanced toward the Nutcracker with his sword raised, Clara pulled off her slipper and threw it at the King! The slipper found its target and the Mouse King fell.

All at once, everything vanished and all that remained where the battle had been, was the Nutcracker who had turned into a handsome prince!

"Come with me, Clara! said the Nutcracker Prince as he whisked her away through the Kingdom of Snow. Snowflakes danced and glistened on the trees.

They arrived at the Land of Sweets, where they were greeted by the Sugar Plum Fairy. The Prince told the Fairy how Clara had saved him from the wicked Mouse King. "We must honor this brave girl," said the Sugar Plum Fairy, as she escorted Clara and the Prince to a candy throne.

Ladies from Spain
and from Arabia danced
in exotic costumes. Clara
was enthralled.

Dancers from around
the world performed for
Clara and the Prince.

Chinese acrobats and swirling
Cossacks held Clara's attention.

Flowers waltzed
with the Sugar
Plum Fairy . . .
what a fantasy!

Floating on a soft cloud, Clara waved goodbye to the Land of Sweets, the Sugar Plum Fairy, and the Nutcracker Prince as they faded from her sight.

Clara awoke in the nursery with the Nutcracker doll still in her arms. Was it all just a lovely dream?

by Andy Rector
Illustrated by Andy Stiles

Grandma Raccoon had a bakery. All day long she baked good things to eat. She baked candies and cakes and pies. Around Christmas Grandma Raccoon would bake Christmas cookies. She made the best Christmas cookies in all the town.

One day Grandma Raccoon put a sign on the window of the bakery. Everyone gathered around to read the sign on the window of the bakery. "Look," said Ernie Squirrel. "The sign says 'Help Wanted.' Let's see if we can help Grandma Raccoon."

They walked into the bakery. They saw Grandma Racoon running around the kitchen. She was out of breath.

"Grandma Raccoon," said Cara Woodchuck, "We came to help."

"Quickly, my friends," said Grandma Raccoon, "Put on your aprons. I need help making Christmas cookies."

"But first," said Grandma Racoon,
"we must move the stove closer to the table.
That way we won't have to run back and
forth as much."

So they pushed the stove. They puffed and panted. The stove was heavy! Finally they pushed it next to the table. "No time to waste!" said Grandma Racoon. "It's time to make Christmas cookies!"

119

Soon they were all busy. Grandma Raccoon measured the flour and sugar. Ernie Squirrel cracked the eggs into the mixing bowl and poured the milk. Cara Woodchuck put sprinkles on cookies that were already baked.

"We are going to give these
cookies to some special people," said
Grandma Raccoon. "Who?" asked Ernie.
Just as Grandma Raccoon was
about to answer, someone walked
into the bakery door.

"Hello, Darnell Deer!" said Grandma Racoon. "I saw your sign," said Darnell. "May I help?"

"Of course," said Grandma Racoon with a smile. "Oh, no," whispered Cara to Ernie. "Darrell Deer is slow and clumsy."

"I know," Ernie whispered back. "He will only get in our way."

Cara Woodchuck and Ernie Squirrel were right. Darnell Deer stepped on everyone's toes. He could not mix the cookie dough because his feet were too big. He bumped into the table and knocked the bag of flour all over the floor.

"I'm sorry," said Darnell. "I guess
I wasn't meant to make cookies."
"Oh, that's okay," said Grandma
Raccoon. "Wait. Something is wrong."
She opened the stove. "The cookies are
not baking. The stove is broken."
"Let me look at the stove," said
Darnell. Darnell Deer looked inside the
stove. He looked on top of the stove.
He looked behind the stove.

"I found the problem," said Darnell.
"The stove is unplugged."
"We must have unplugged it when we moved the stove," said Grandma Racoon.
Everyone laughed. Grandma Racoon plugged the stove into a closer outlet.
"Now friends," she said.
"Let's finish the cookies."

The next day was Christmas.
Grandma Raccoon and her friends took
the Christmas cookies to the special
people that Grandma talked about.
Who were they? They were sick children
in the hospital. Darnell carried the
big sack of cookies while the others
passed them out to the children.
"Thanks for all your help, Darnell,"
said Grandma Raccoon.
"You've made this a wonderful Christmas."

Frosty the Snowman

During the night, the first big snow of the winter had fallen. The next morning was bright and sunny. The children came out of their houses and began to roll balls of snow. They had two large snowballs in no time.

After placing one large snowball on top of the other, the children rolled a third snowball that was just the right size for a head. Tommy brought pieces of coal for the eyes and a button for the nose. "Here's a straw broom for him to carry," said Karen.

"These old rubber boots will be great for the snowman," said Jimmy.

"He can wear my old mittens and scarf," giggled Lindsay.

"All he needs now is a hat," the children agreed. Karen found an old ball cap, but it just wouldn't stay on the snowman's head.

Tommy tried an old, tattered hat that his dad wore fishing, but that wasn't right either.

The wind began to whistle and blow. As if by magic, a shiny, black top hat came blowing across the snow-covered yard and came to rest at the children's feet. Lindsay reached down, picked up the hat, and placed it on the snowman's head.

All at once, the snowman began to speak! "Hi, boys and girls! I'm Frosty the Snowman." he said.

That is how the adventures of Frosty the Snowman began.

Having a snowman as your special friend makes the winter days even more fun. The children's sleds coasted down the hills faster than ever before. Their snow fort was the best they had ever built.

Ice skating on the pond was never this much fun before. Amazingly, the children didn't get cold and shivery with Frosty nearby. They weren't sure if it was the warmth of Frosty's heart or the magic of his smile. It didn't matter why . . . they were having a wonderful time.

Each day, Frosty surprised the children with an exciting, new adventure. "I've never seen a store," Frosty told the children one day. "I'd like to go shopping," he grinned. "What a great idea!" exclaimed Lindsay. "I know where there is a great toy store," added Tommy. Singing merrily, they started towards town.

TOYS

Frosty and the children loved to look into the brightly decorated store windows. Their eyes were wide with excitement! The children led Frosty all round the streets of town in the warm, winter sunshine.

Frosty and the children were on a busy 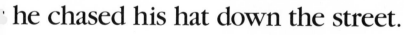 street corner where a policeman was directing traffic. Suddenly, a warm gust of wind blew Frosty's hat into the street!

The policeman whistled the children to stop. They were unable to follow Frosty he chased his hat down the street.

As soon as the traffic light turned green, the children raced down the street to find Frosty. His shiny, black top hat was still rolling through the melted snow, but there was no Frosty!

"Frosty the Snowman is gone!
Do you know
where he is?" the children asked the policeman.

"When the winter sun is warm
and bright, all snowmen disappear.
But Frosty will be back again with
a cold and snowy day," answered
the policeman.

And you know . . . the policeman is right! Frosty will be back again someday soon!

Santa Has the Sniffles!

by Diane Stortz
Illustrated by Rocky Katz

Christmas Eve was only two nights away--
and Santa Claus was sick! "Say ahhhhh," said
the doctor, as he looked down Santa's throat.
"Ears hurting? Head throbbing? Eyes
watering? Muscles aching?" "Ah-ah-ah-CHOO!"
said Santa. "Bless you," said the doctor, and he
handed Santa a tissue.

"Santa has the sniffles," the doctor told Mrs. Claus. "He needs to stay in bed and drink plenty of juice. He should be feeling better in about a week."

"Christmas Eve is only two nights away!" said Santa. "The children will think I've forgotten Christmas. They will think I've forgotten *them*! Ah-ah-ah-CHOO!" "I *am* sorry," said the doctor. "But you can't travel around the world in an open sleigh with such a serious case of the sniffles."

Santa closed his eyes to take a nap.
Mrs. Claus closed the door to Santa's room
and hurried to the elves' workshop.

All the elves stopped working when they saw Mrs. Claus. "Santa has the sniffles," Mrs. Claus said. "He won't be able to fly his sleigh on Christmas Eve unless we do something to help him."

The elves thought. . . and thought . . . and thought. . . until finally one little elf named Elvin jumped up and shouted, "I've got it!" Mrs. Claus and all the elves came closer to hear Elvin's plan.

On Christmas Eve, the elves knocked on Santa's door. "Come in, dear elves," said Mrs. Claus.

"Dear Santa," said Elvin, "we sent a message to children everywhere that you have the sniffles. We told the children that Christmas will be a little late this year. And look! Instead of letters asking for toys, the children have sent you get-well cards! And we have made you some very special soup."

"Ho! Ho! Ho!" chuckled Santa. "Ah-CHOO!" He read all the cards and had a big bowl of soup. "Thank you, elves," said Santa. "I feel so much better now. In fact, I think I have stopped sneezing. I don't think Christmas will have to be late after all!"

"Hurray!" shouted the elves and Mrs. Claus. The elves filled Santa's sleigh with toys and Christmas packages. Elvin gave each reindeer a carrot and an extra lump of sugar. Mrs. Claus made a steaming jug of hot cocoa and helped Santa into his suit. Then Santa climbed into his sleigh, and off he flew!"

At house after house, Santa filled stockings and piled presents under the tree. He never sneezed once.

But at the very last house on Santa's list, a little dog sleeping on a little boy's bed pricked up his ears. He thought he had heard someone sneeze.

A Christmas Carol

From the story
by
CHARLES DICKENS

Scrooge was a mean, old miser who didn't care for anyone or anything . . . except his money.

He disliked everything. Most of all, he hated Christmas. When someone would wish him a "Merry Christmas," he would grumble, "Bah, humbug!"

Poor Bob Cratchit was working late for Scrooge again. He very much wanted to go home to his family. After all, it was Christmas Eve.

Finally, old Scrooge allowed Cratchit to leave. "Would you like to spend Christmas with my family?" he asked Scrooge.

"Nonsense! Christmas, bah humbug! Now leave me alone. I have work to do!" Scrooge answered.

Late that night, Mr. Scrooge went home to his dark house. As he got to his door, the knocker appeared to turn into the face of his partner, Jacob Marley, who had died years ago.

Frightened, Scrooge hurried inside and went straight to his bedroom. He changed into his nightshirt and crawled into bed.

"Ebenezer Scrooo-ooge!" a voice cried out in the dark room. Suddenly a ghost appeared, covered in locks and chains!

"Marley, why do you haunt me?" said Scrooge, shaking with fright.

"To save you from yourself, Ebenezer!" the ghost cried "Tonight you will be visited by three spirits who will show you the *true* meaning of Christmas!"

"Ghosts and spirits indeed!" growled Scrooge as he drifted off to sleep.

As the clock struck one o'clock, the first of three spirits appeared.

"Ebenezer Scrooo-ooge," a voice called. "I am the Ghost of Christmas Past," said the spirit. "Come with me."

"Where are we?" asked Scrooge.

"Have you forgotten your childhood, Ebenezer?" asked the spirit.

"Why this is my old schoolhouse," Scrooge said with surprise.

"Yes, Ebenezer. That little child sitting alone is you. Many a Christmas you spent alone without friends or family," said the spirit. "Money became your only joy and love."

Scrooge saw himself as a young man again. Beside him was a woman, Belle. "I had almost forgotten how beautiful she was," Scrooge sighed.

"You were to marry her, remember?" asked the spirit. "But gold was more important to you."

"No! Spirit, take me away. Forgive me, Belle!" cried Scrooge.

When Scrooge looked up, he was back in his room and the spirit was gone.

"Ebenezer Scrooo-ooge!" called a voice.

"Come closer," the spirit roared. "I am the Ghost of Christmas Present. Come with me, you have a great deal to learn tonight."

"Who's little house is this?" asked Scrooge. "This is the house of your clerk, Bob Cratchit," answered the spirit.

The spirit pointed to the door. In the doorway was Bob, with his son, Tiny Tim, high upon his shoulder.

"Merry Christmas!" Bob called to his family as he hugged his wife.

"And how's our Tiny Tim?" asked Bob. "I believe he's getting stronger every day."

"Of course he is," Mrs. Cratchit said, holding back a tear as Tiny Tim hobbled to his stool.

"I didn't know the child was sick," said Scrooge.

"Would you have cared, Ebenezer?" asked the spirit.

"Spirit," said Scrooge. "Tell me, will Tiny Tim live?"

"I see an empty stool and a crutch in the corner. If these shadows remain unchanged, the child will die."

"No, spirit," Scrooge begged. "Don't let the boy die!"

"It is not by my kindness that he will live, but by yours, Ebenezer . . . if you *truly* care. Come now!" said the spirit.

Scrooge traveled with the spirit to see many families, both rich and poor, to see the love and joy of the Christmas spirit that night.

"Before you leave, tell me spirit, what is that I see moving beneath your robe?" asked Scrooge. The spirit opened his robe and clinging to his legs were two small children: a small, ragged boy and a forlorn, little girl. "Are they yours Spirit?" asked Scrooge.

"This boy is *Ignorance.* This girl is *Want.* Beware them both," the spirit said sadly, then disappeared.

187

Scrooge stood shivering in the new-fallen snow. He turned to find himself before a dark and gloomy spirit.

"Are you the Ghost of Christmas Yet to Come?" asked Scrooge. The spirit said nothing, but nodded in reply.

The spirit fixed his eyes upon Scrooge, then pointed a bony finger toward the mist.

"Lead on, spirit," moaned Scrooge.

The spirit said nothing. Scrooge then saw what he dreaded most . . . the empty stool and the little crutch of Tiny Tim.

"No, spirit no!" Scrooge cried out. "Tell me it isn't so."

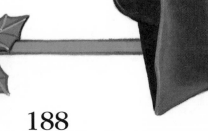

Scrooge began to weep. As he raised his head, he found he was in a graveyard. The spirit was pointing to a tombstone.

Scrooge drew close to the grave. There on the headstone was his name, EBENEZER SCROOGE.

"No, spirit! I will be a better man! Please! No, no!" Scrooge suddenly awoke on Christmas morning to find himself back in his own bed. The spirits had done their work in one night! Excitedly, Scrooge ran to the window and threw open the shutters.

"Merry Christmas!" shouted Scrooge. Then, as he spotted a passing boy, he called out, "Boy! Hurry! Go down the street and buy the big turkey that hangs in the butcher's shop and take it to Bob Cratchit's house!" He tossed a large bag of gold coins down to the boy.

"Friends are worth more than all the gold in the world," said Scrooge. From then on, he made sure Bob Cratchit and his family had all the good food and warm clothing they needed.

After that night, Scrooge became a better man and kept the spirit of Christmas alive.

Marla's
Toyshop Adventure

by Andy Rector
Illustrated by Tim Bowers

Marla Mouse was trying to sleep.
"What is all that noise?" she said. "I can't sleep."

Marla opened her front door. She saw elves everywhere!

The elves hammered nails into wood. They dropped paint cans on the floor with a thud. They talked and talked with excitement in their voices. No wonder Marla could not sleep! Marla watched them all evening. Finally the elves left their toyshop. All the toys were made.

The elves had made many toys! Marla walked out of her mouse hole. She wanted to explore.

Marla found a top. She spun it. She found another top. She spun it, too. She found a third top. She spun it, too. She had three tops spinning at once.

Marla found a tea set. She had tea with the Queen.

Marla played electronic football. She danced on the buttons and made a touchdown.

What was that noise? thought Marla. She looked around. A cat! Marla jumped into a toy car and drove away.

Marla escaped into a big doll house. In the bedroom she found a bed. She slept safely in a doll bed hidden from the cat.

The next morning Marla woke up and heard a voice. "Someone has been playing with the toys!" Marla ran out of the doll house. She saw Santa Claus. "Santa," said Marla. "Let me help you give these toys to children. I want them to have as much fun as I did."

That night was Christmas Eve. The Elves packed Santa's toy bag. Santa Claus and Marla rode all night giving toys to children all over the world. Marla never forgot that wonderful Christmas!

The Little Drummer Boy

Classic Holiday Collection

written by Dandi
illustrated by Tammie Speer-Lyon

The boy tapped on his drum as he watched the camels drink. He wondered where the three wise men were going that starry night.

Po-rum-pum-pum-pum, he played. The little Drummer Boy had made the drum himself from animal skin and a piece of an old hollow log. *Rum-pum-pum-pum*. To his ears, his music on the drum sounded like the sound the camels made as they drank.

Finally the three wise men came out, their robes trailing behind them. "Are the camels ready?" asked the first.

The boy hid his drum behind his back. He didn't want them to think he wasn't doing his job. "They are ready, Sirs," he said.

"It's a fine night for a journey," said the second wise man.

The Drummer Boy could stand it no longer. "Tell me he pleaded. "Where are you going?"

"We're following that star," said the third wise man, pointing to the brightest star in the sky.

The Drummer Boy watched them load a heavy box of gold onto the first camel. Next came a jar of fragrant frankincense, then precious myrrh.

"Why do you carry gifts?" asked the Drummer Boy.

"The star will lead us to the newborn King," said the first wise man.

"Please, let me come with you," begged the Drummer Boy. And the wise men agreed.

The Drummer Boy fell in behind the three wise men. As the camels' hooves went clippity-clop, the boy played his drum: *Rat-tat-ta-tat*. He was on his way to see the newborn King.

Suddenly the Drummer Boy had a terrible thought! He wanted to give something wonderful to the child, but he had nothing to give. He owned nothing that could please a king.

Day after day they traveled on. The Drummer Boy kept the camels moving with his steady drumming: *Da-da-drum-drum*.

The star led them all the way to Bethlehem to a manger. The three wise men knelt before the baby and presented their gifts of gold, frankincense, and myrrh.

But the little Drummer Boy waited outside. How could he go in without a gift?

Suddenly the Drummer Boy heard a cry. He peeked into the stable. The sheep pushed at their stall. Oxen pawed the ground. Donkeys brayed. And the baby cried.

The baby's mother, Mary, looked directly into the face of the little Drummer Boy.

"Shall I play for him?" the boy asked softly. Mary nodded.

Slowly the Drummer Boy began to play.
Pa-rum-pum-pum-pum. The ox and lambs kept time.
Pa-rum-pum-pum-pum.

The Drummer Boy drew nearer to
Baby Jesus. 'I'll play my best for
him,' he thought.
Pa-rum-pum-pum-pum.
Rum-pum-pum-pum,
Rum-pum-pum-pum.
On his drum.

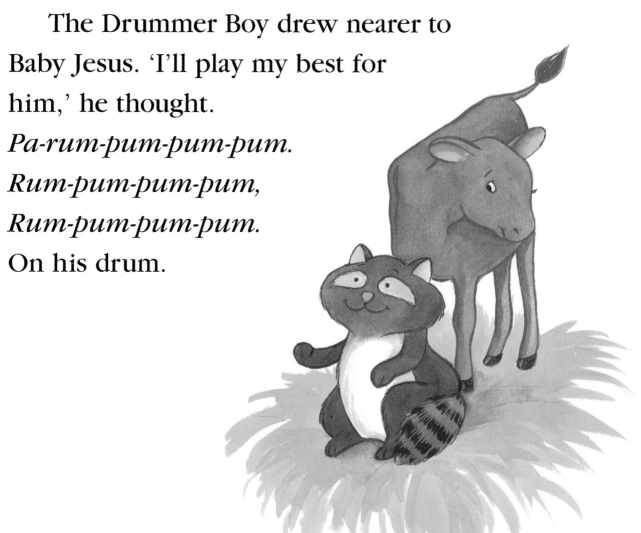

By the time the Drummer Boy finished, Baby Jesus had stopped crying.

The little Drummer Boy gently lay down his drum beside the manger. And when he looked in, he was sure the newborn King's smile was just for him.

The
Always-Late Angel

by Diane Stortz
Illustrated by Joe Stites

Once there was a little angel who was always late for choir practice.

When she should have been singing with the heavenly choir, she was usually out gathering sunbeams,

riding on a comet, or swinging on a star.

That's where she was when Gabriel told the angel choir that baby Jesus would soon be born on earth.

"We are all going to earth to sing the good news!" said Gabriel. Every angel was excited, and off they all flew.

When the little angel remembered that she was supposed to be at choir practice, she hurried back to heaven. But she was too late. She couldn't hear any singing. "Where are all the angels in the angel choir?" she asked the gatekeeper.

"Why, they've gone to earth to sing the good news that baby Jesus has been born," said the gatekeeper.

"Oh, my goodness!" said the little angel. " I'd better try to catch up with them!"

But she was too late. The angel choir had already sung their heavenly songs and gone back to heaven. All the little angel could see were some sleepy sheep.

"I wonder where I should go now," said the little angel.

"Baaaa," said a sheep.

"To Bethlehem!" said the little angel, and she hurried toward the little town.

In the quiet streets of Bethlehem the little angel saw some shepherds. They were talking about a baby they had seen in a stable!

The little angel flew over Bethlehem, looking for the stable. "I see it!" she said. Inside the stable were Mary and Joseph and baby Jesus.

The little angel tiptoed to the baby's bed. Baby Jesus looked up at her and smiled. Then the little angel sang him a heavenly song. She hadn't been late for Christmas after all!

Santa Claus
Is Coming To Town

written by Dandi
illustrated by Tammie Speer-Lyon

Max kicked at a snow bank as he watched his big sister, Jennifer, play with her friends. Why couldn't she play with him? Finally he shouted, "Jennifer! I want to make a snowman NOW!

"Don't shout, Max," Jennifer called to him. And she went back to her snowball fight.

Max didn't understand. Why shouldn't he shout outside where the snow could swallow his shout?

Max plopped down on the step to pout. Just then, a stray snowball landed smack on Max's nose!

"Mom!" he cried, running into the house. "A snowball hi me!" Max told his mother. And although it didn't really hurt Max started to cry. Max's mother kissed him.

"Better not cry," she said gently.

"Shall I tell you why?"

Now Max *was* confused! He tried to think.

You better not shout. . .
You better not pout. . .
Better not cry. . .
I'm telling you why. . .

Max remembered.

"Santa Claus!" he shouted.

Then in a whisper, "Santa
Claus is coming to town.

Max knew he
probably hadn't made
Santa's list of good boys
and girls this year. Take
the time his cousin slept over.

Max kicked him out of bed.

Not exactly *nice*.

When Max had watered Mother's flowers
with juice, it had seemed funny. . .

until the flowers died. That wasn't
so nice either.

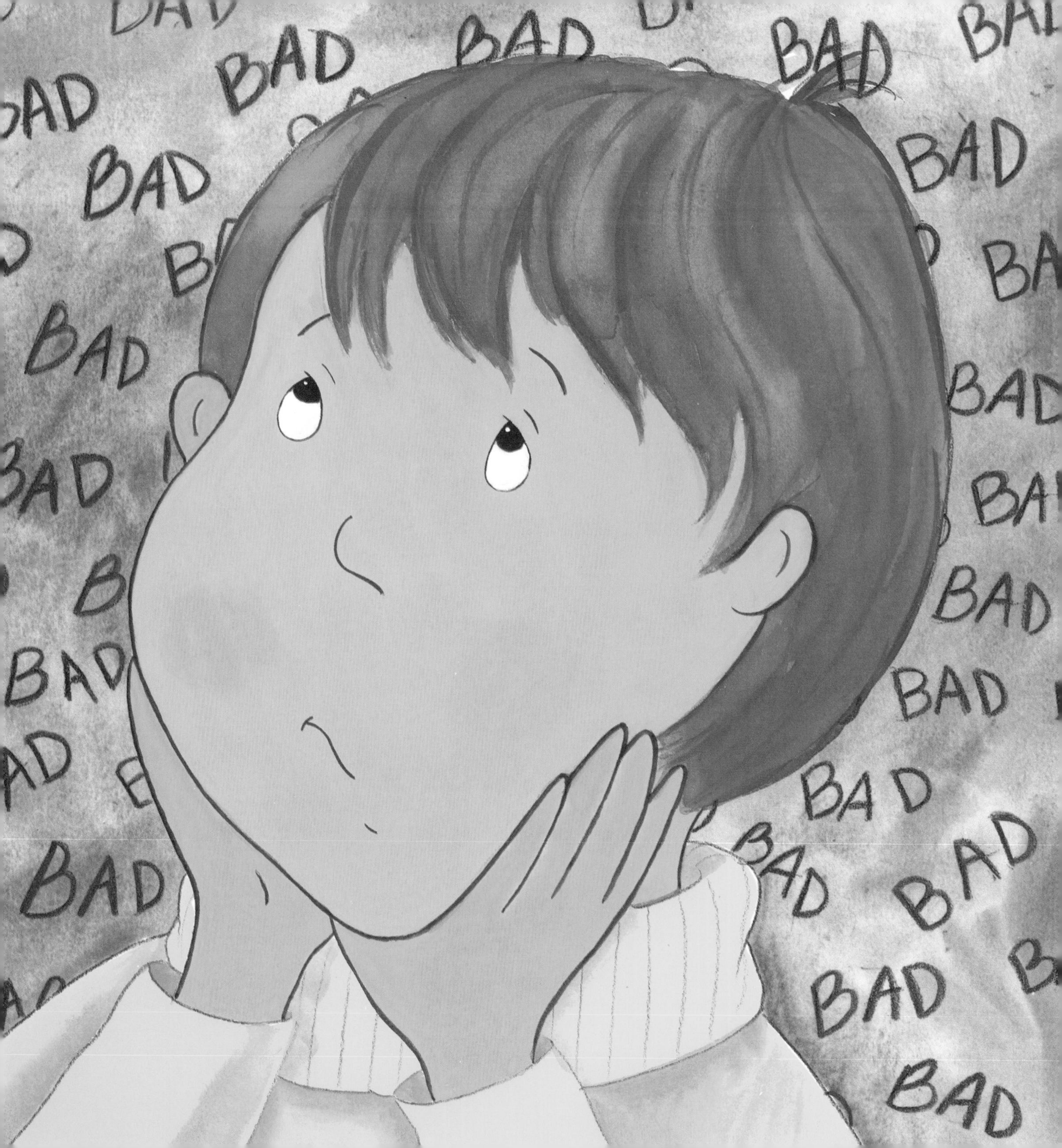
BAD
BAD
BAD
BAD
BAD
BAD
BAD
BAD
BAD
BAD
BAD
BAD
BAD
BAD

"Jennifer," Max asked when she came in, "Do you think I've been naughty or nice this year?"

"Well," Jennifer said, grinning. "You did stick gum in my hair while I was sleeping. It sure didn't *feel* nice when Mom had to cut it out."

Max had to face it. Santa Claus might be coming to town, but he probably wouldn't stop at Max's stocking.

Christmas Eve, Max and Jennifer put tinsel on the tree. "Tonight's the night Santa Claus is coming to town," Jennifer said. "Aren't you excited, Max!" But Max knew he had been more naughty than nice this year. Santa wouldn't leave anything for him.

Max imagined Santa and his reindeer flying from house to house. It would be hard work carrying that pouch down so many chimneys. Santa must get awfully tired. "Mom," Max called, "Could I have some milk and cookies, please?"

"It's awfully late," Mother answered.

"They're not for me," said Max. Max set out a big glass of cold milk and four Christmas cookies he had decorated himself.

Max woke up first on Christmas morning. He crept downstairs in darkness, afraid to look at his stocking. He knew it would be empty.

Light from the treetop angel fell on the mantel. There, to his surprise, Max saw his own Christmas stocking bulging with gifts from Santa. Sticking out at the top was a note:

Dear Max,

Thanks for the treat!

What you did was very nice!

Merry Christmas!

Love,

Santa

280

"I was NICE!" Max shouted. And he ran through the house, waking up his family, singing:

"He made up his list, and checked it all twice.
Santa decided Max could be nice!
Santa Claus is coming to town."

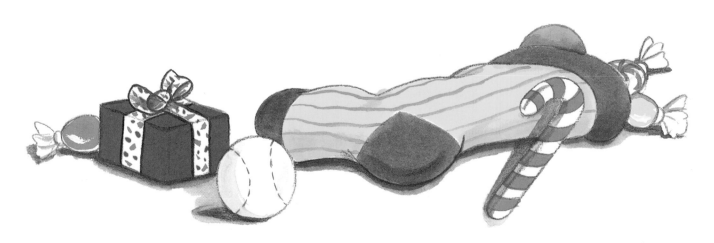

Teddy's Christmas Surprise

by Diane Stortz

Illustrated by Tim Bowers

Every year on December 1, Mother Bear said, "Time to get ready for Christmas!" So Mother Bear and Father Bear and Teddy Bear and Teddy's twin sisters swept and scrubbed and polished,

and hung pine garland and twinkling lights, and put candles in the windows and a wreath on the front door.

They decorated the Christmas tree and made cookies and candy to give to all their neighbors.

Then they planned the presents they would give to one another. Father made his presents in his workshop. Mother made her presents in her sewing room. And the twins went shopping at the mall. "I want to give presents too," said Teddy. "I'm big enough." "All right," said Mother. "Will you need any help?" "No," said Teddy. "I want my presents to be a Christmas surprise."

Teddy took down his piggy bank and shook it to see how much money he had. He didn't have any. "Then I will make my presents," said Teddy.

Teddy looked in Mother's craft closet. He looked in Mother's craft books. He tried very hard to follow the directions.

But Teddy's presents didn't turn out
very well. "Now what will I do?" said
Teddy. "What will I give for my Christmas
surprise?"

One day right before Christmas, Grandma Bear came to stay with Teddy while Mother Bear ran some last-minute errands and the twins were at school. Suddenly, Teddy knew exactly what his Christmas surprise would be!

On Christmas morning, Mother Bear gave Father Bear a quilted vest, and Father Bear gave Mother Bear a nice spice rack. Mother Bear gave striped overalls to Teddy, and Father Bear gave Teddy a toy train that tooted.

The twins got warm-up suits from Mother Bear and jewelry boxes from Father Bear. They gave a picture of themselves to Mother and Father Bear, roller skates to Teddy, and hair bows to each other.

"Where is your Christmas surprise, Teddy?" asked Mother Bear. "Come close and I will show you," said Teddy.

He gave everyone in his family a big Christmas bear hug!

Santa's Toy Shop

Classic Holiday Collection

written by Dandi
illustrated by Tammie Speer-Lyon

Santa's toy shop buzzed with activity. Only two days until Christmas Eve, when Santa would load the presents in his sleigh and deliver them to children around the world!

Elves hammered nails in rocking horses and doll houses. Even Mrs. Santa Claus helped. She sat by a

snow-framed window and put the last stitches in a brand new baseball.

Ellie, the youngest of Santa's helpers, sat in a pile of wrapping paper. She wanted to do her best wrapping gifts.

Then, maybe Santa would let her be a toy maker next Christmas. How she would love to make dolls and bikes and toy cars!

"Santa," Ellie said as she tucked in another gift "I'm worried."

"Only two days left and still no letter from Danny. How will I know what gift to wrap for him?"

"You must do your best, Ellie," Santa said.

315

"Mail call!" Mrs. Claus shouted from the window.
"Here comes Elf Edward on Blitzen."

Edward handed the letters to Santa.

"Ellie!" Santa called. "There's a letter from Danny.
He wants a skateboard."

"That was close!" said Ellie. She picked a bright green skateboard from the elf assembly line. Next she wrapped the skateboard and stuffed it into Santa's pouch.

Now it was the day before Christmas
Eve. Elves put a last minute shine
on trumpets and trains. Shiny shoes
got new laces. Other elves tried
out the latest computer games.
Ellie wrapped and wrapped.

Just then the door to the toy shop
burst open, nearly knocking Santa down.
"Well, upon my whiskers, Edward!"
said Santa.

"Sorry, Santa,"
cried Edward. "I knew you'd want
to see this right away!" He handed
Santa another letter from Danny.

320

Ellie tried to look over Santa's shoulder as he read:

Dear Santa,
I told Mom about the skateboard. She said
"NO WAY!" Would you please bring me
a ten-speed bike instead?"
        Love,
            DANNY

Ellie rushed to Santa's pouch and dumped it on the toy shop floor. She pulled out the skateboard, wrapped a Blue racing bike, and stuffed it into the bag. It wasn't easy!

Christmas Eve day the elves groomed the reindeer. Mrs. Claus packed Santa a midnight snack. And Ellie sat alone in the workshop tieing bows on the last packages.

This time it was Santa who burst in with another letter from Danny:

Dear Santa,
I'm really not big enough for a ten-speed.
I thought about asking for one of your
reindeer, but you need them. So if it's not
too much trouble, please just surprise me.
            Your friend,
            DANNY

"Now what am I supposed to do, Santa?" Ellie asked.

"Do your best, Little Elf," Santa said. "Think. What would you want for Christmas?"

All Ellie ever wanted was to make toys. Maybe Danny liked to make things too. . .

Ellie wrapped a tool box with a toy hammer and tools, and loaded it in Santa's sleigh. "I hope Danny likes this," she whispered to Rudolph.

While Santa delivered presents, Ellie swept the toy shop and worried. 'If Danny doesn't like his gift, I may never get to be a toy maker.'

Christmas Day, another letter arrived. "It's from Danny!" Santa cried. Ellie held her breath and listened.

Dear Santa,
Thank you so much for the tool box. It was exactly what I wanted!
        Love, DANNY

"Yippee!" Ellie and the other elves cheered. "Well, I'll be a red-nosed reindeer!" exclaimed Santa. "Looks like we'll have a new toy maker named Ellie next Christmas!"

Semour Seal's Christmas Present

by Andy Rector

Illustrated by Kora Oliver

Semour Seal saw the other seal pups swimming. They were having a Christmas swimming party. "Jump in the water, Semour" they called to him. But Semour would not jump into the water.

"Why don't you jump into the water?" someone asked Semour. Semour turned around to see who was talking. He saw a polar bear. "Who are you?" asked Semour. "I am Peter,' said the polar bear.

"Now tell me why you won't jump into the water," said Peter. Semour said, "I am afraid of the water. I won't be able to join the other seal pups for the Christmas swimming party."

"Afraid?" said Peter. "Afraid of the water?" Peter thought for a minute. "I have an idea" he said to Semour. "Jump on my tummy."

Suddenly Peter slid down a snow slide. Semour hung on to Peter's fur. Down, down, down they slid. "This is fun!" said Semour.

Splash! The snow slide ended and Peter floated on the water. Semour saw water all around him. "This is not fun anymore!" he said.

"Jump into the water" said Peter. "I'll keep you safe" Semour was afraid, but he trusted Peter. Semour jumped off Peter's tummy. He began to swim!

"I can swim!" said Semour. "Of course" said Peter. "All seals can swim," Semour swam under water. He swam almost to the ocean floor. Peter followed him.

Semour saw something on the ocean floor. It was a treasure chest! He pointed the chest out to Peter. Peter dragged the treasure chest to the surface.

They opened it. Beautiful jewels filled the treasure chest! Diamonds, rubies, and other precious gems shone with beautiful colors. "What is that?" the other seal pups asked as they gathered around the treasure chest.

"Let's give them each a gem as a Christmas present," said Semour to Peter. And they did. "There are no more gems," said Peter after the last seal pup left. Now we have no presents to give each other."

"You already gave me a present," said Semour. "You taught me to swim." "And you have given me the best gift of all," said Peter. "Friendship. Merry Christmas."